Note to parents, carers and teachers

Read it yourself is a series of modern stories, favourite characters and traditional tales written in a simple way for children who are learning to read. The books can be read independently or as part of a guided reading session.

Each book is carefully structured to include many high-frequency words vital for first reading. The sentences on each page are supported closely by pictures to help with understanding, and to offer lively details to talk about.

The books are graded into four levels that progressively introduce wider vocabulary and longer stories as a reader's ability and confidence grows.

Ideas for use

- Begin by looking through the book and talking about the pictures. Has your child heard this story before?

- Help your child with any words he does not know, either by helping him to sound them out or supplying them yourself.

- Developing readers can be concentrating so hard on the words that they sometimes don't fully grasp the meaning of what they're reading. Answering the puzzle questions on pages 30 and 31 will help with understanding.

For more information and advice on Read it yourself and book banding, visit www.ladybird.com/readityourself

Book
Band
6

Level 2 is ideal for children who have received some reading instruction and can read short, simple sentences with help.

Special features:

Frequent repetition of main story words and phrases

Short, simple sentences

Large, clear type

Careful match between story and pictures

The first little pig built his house of straw.

The second little pig built his house of sticks.

The third little pig built his house of bricks.

8

"Then I'll huff and I'll puff and I'll blow your house down," said the big, bad wolf.

And he huffed and he puffed and he blew the house down!

14

15

Educational Consultant: Geraldine Taylor
Book Banding Consultant: Kate Ruttle

A catalogue record for this book is available from the British Library

Published by Ladybird Books Ltd
80 Strand, London, WC2R 0RL
A Penguin Company

001

ISBN: 978-0-72327-294-6

Printed in Italy by G. Canale & C. S.p.A. – Borgaro T.se (TO)

The Three
Little Pigs

Illustrated by Virginia Allyn

Once upon a time,
there were three little pigs.

One day, they went out
to build their own houses.

The first little pig built
his house of straw.

The second little pig
built his house of sticks.

The third little pig built
his house of bricks.

Along came a big, bad
wolf. He went up to the
house of straw.

"Little pig, little pig,
let me come in,"
said the big, bad wolf.

But the first little pig
said, "By the hair of
my chinny, chin, chin,
I will not let you in!"

"Then I'll huff and I'll puff and I'll blow your house down," said the big, bad wolf.

And he huffed and he puffed and he blew the house down!

The big, bad wolf went up
to the house of sticks.

"Little pig, little pig,
let me come in," he said.

But the second little pig said, "By the hair of my chinny, chin, chin, I will not let you in!"

"Then I'll huff and I'll puff and I'll blow your house down," said the big, bad wolf.

And he huffed and he puffed and he blew the house down!

The big, bad wolf went up
to the house of bricks.

"Little pig, little pig,
let me come in," he said.

But the third little pig said, "By the hair of my chinny, chin, chin, I will not let you in!"

"Then I'll huff and I'll puff and I'll blow your house down," said the big, bad wolf.

So he huffed and he puffed and he huffed and he puffed, but he could not blow the house down.

The big, bad wolf climbed on top of the house and came down the chimney...

SPLASH!

That was the end of
the big, bad wolf!

How much do you remember about the story of The Three Little Pigs? Answer these questions and find out!

- What is the first little pig's house made of?

- What do the three little pigs say to the big, bad wolf when he wants to come in?

- What happens when the big, bad wolf tries to blow down the house of bricks?

- How do the three little pigs trick the big, bad wolf?

Look at the pictures and match the pigs to their houses. Can you spot the big, bad wolf?

bricks

sticks

straw

Read it yourself with Ladybird

Tick the books you've read!

For beginner readers who can read short, simple sentences with help.

Level 2

 Beauty and the Beast ☐

 Chicken Licken ☐

 Little Red Riding Hood ☐

 Nature Trail ☐

 Sports Day ☐

 Pirate School ☐

 Rumpelstiltskin ☐

 Sleeping Beauty ☐

 The Gingerbread Man ☐

 Sly Fox and Red Hen ☐

 The Tale of Jemima Puddle-Duck ☐

 The Three Little Pigs ☐

 Why Lion Roarrrs! ☐

 The Big Race ☐

 Town Mouse and Country Mouse ☐

 Dom's Dragon ☐

For more confident readers who can read simple stories with help.

Level 3

 YOU won't like this present as much as I DO! ☐

 The Elves and the Shoemaker ☐

 Hansel and Gretel ☐

 Harry and the Bucketful of Dinosaurs ☐

 Jack and the Beanstalk ☐

 Furi on Music Island ☐

 Poppet Stows Away ☐

 Rapunzel ☐

 The Red Knight ☐

 Available on the App Store

The Read it yourself with Ladybird app is now available for iPad, iPhone and iPod touch

App also available on Android devices